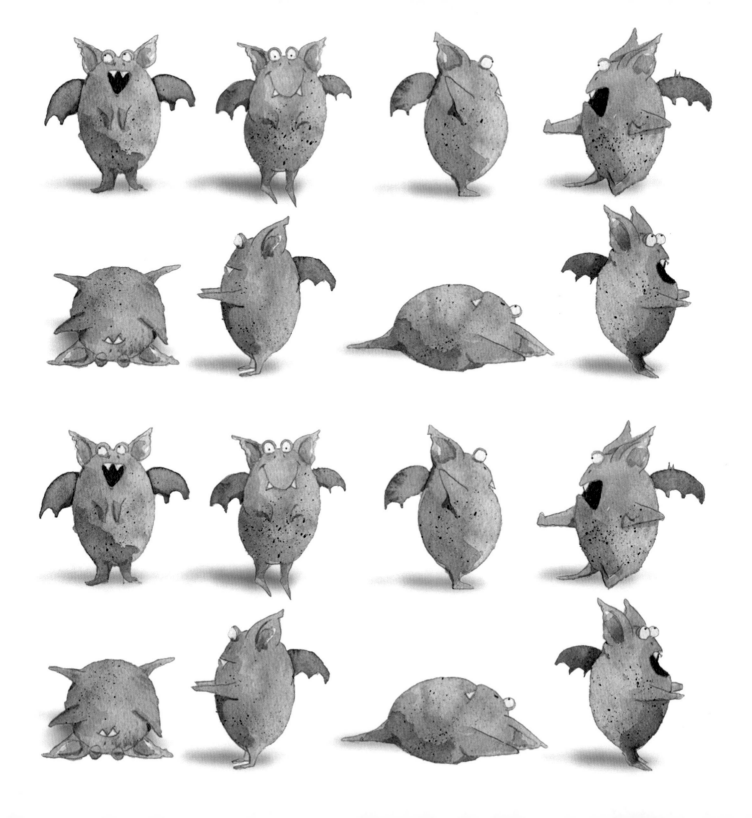

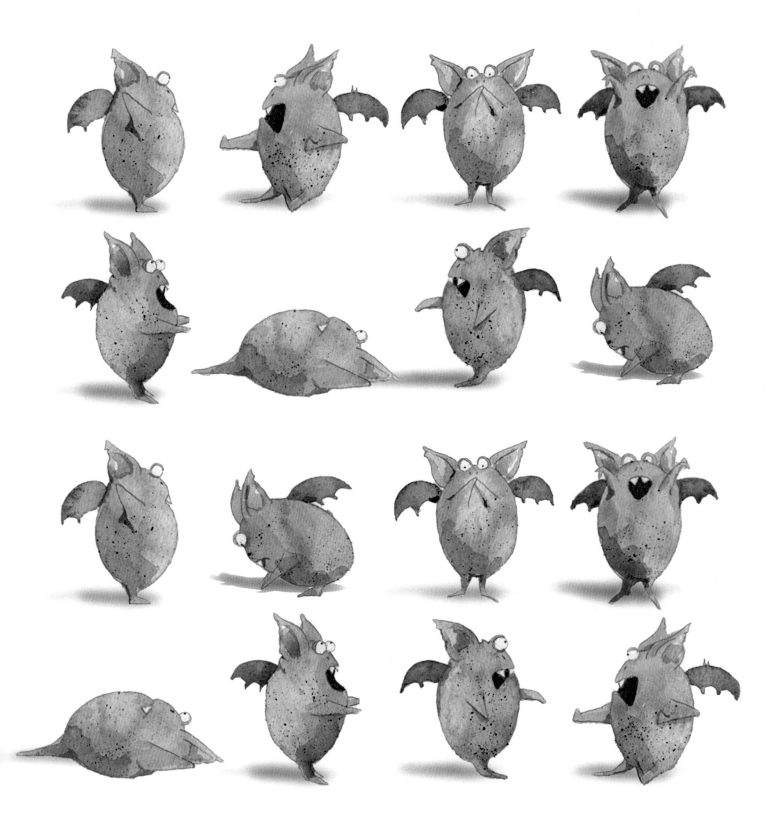

To Marco and Marin.
And to you brave and gentle souls.
In a world full of fear and unrest, a kind act
can change everything.
P.M.

FOR THE LOVE OF HALLOWEEN

One Scary Old Ghost Story

by P. Marin

There once roamed a ghost. A very old ghost. So old that when Halloween came, he itched for that creeping hour when bats wake and witches ride off into the raven-black sky. All so he could curl up with his blanket for a good night's rest.

The old ghost soaked

and snuggled

and tucked.

But as the sun sank into the belly of the gloomy, dark night, an unwelcome lot came knocking.

"Knock, knock,"

banged the beastly bunch, clamoring at the foot of his porch.
"Oh, rats and bats," he groaned, throwing back the covers. He thumped and mumbled down the stairs.

10 vile vampires, 9 moaning mummies, and 8 pesky witches with tall, pointed hats all chanted,

"TRICK OR TREAT!"

"For the love of wretched spleen stew, stop knocking at my door," the old ghost grumbled.

He threw lizards and innards into their sacks, then slammed the door shut.

From where his toes were not to where his chin should have been, he tucked himself in, then nuzzled ever so wearily into his fuzzy down pillow. Before the first drop of drool could fall, he was bothered and downright pestered by the "KNOCK, KNOCK," rising from below.

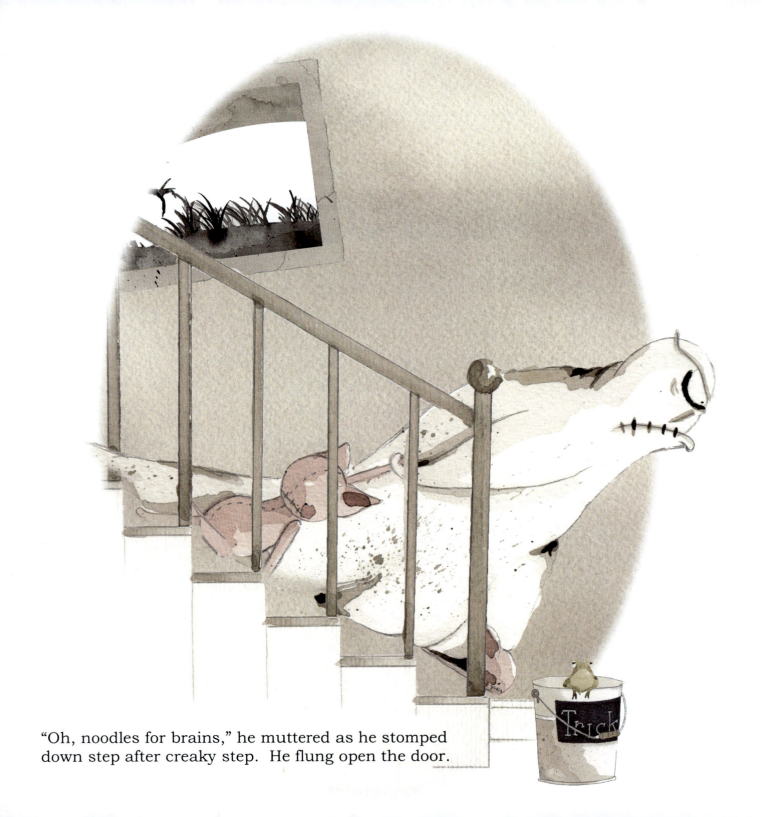

"Oh, noodles for brains," he muttered as he stomped down step after creaky step. He flung open the door.

7 eerie trolls, 6 bony skeletons, and 5 feral cats screeched,

"TRICK OR TREAT!"

Into their bags he tossed warty toads and leftover eyeballs.
"For the love of slimy, green goo," the old ghost roared. "Stop knocking at my door!"

Slamming the door, he shook his head and floated back to bed. Before his snore could shake that rickety, run-down shack, he sat straight up and hollered, "Who's knocking at my door?!?"

"FOR THE LOVE OF HALLOWEEN," the old ghost cried,

BOO!

4 ghastly ghouls, 3 screaming zombies, and 2 rotten goblins ran trembling into the night.

Then there, under the fullest of moons, wrapped in that grim, crisp Halloween sky, there was 1.

One scary, old ghost,
fast asleep.

For the Love of Halloween: One Scary Old Ghost Story

Copyright © 2021 by P. Marin

All rights reserved.

Library of Congress Control Number: 2021906221

Prints Marin, Ink, Huntington Beach, CA

P. Marin

For the Love of Halloween: One Scary Old Ghost Story.

ISBN-10: 0-9986110-3-X   ISBN-13: 978-0-9986119-3-8

I. Title   II. Series

$E = mc^2$ Fear. It's relative.

FIND THE FEAR

Inside FOR THE LOVE OF HALLOWEEN I've drawn some things I'm afraid of. Can you find them?

1. Bats
2. Lizards
3. Warty toads
4. Innards
5. Leftover eyeballs
6. People running with sharp objects
7. Haunted house
8. Math and numbers
9. Ghosts
10. Vampires
11. Mummies
12. Skeletons
14. Witches
15. Trolls
16. Ghouls
17. Goblins
18. Zombies
19. Someone yelling "BOO!"
20. Feeling different or left out
21. Making mistakes

You should know, even though I have a lot of fears, I never let them keep me from doing what I love. Ever.

Now tell me, what are you afraid of?

PRINTS MARIN, INK
Find What You Love and Do It Often.
printsmarin.com

Many Halloween moons ago, I was telling our son a bedtime story. "There once lived a ghost, a very old ghost, so old that when Halloween came..."

In the middle of the story, our son stopped me and said, "This is really good. You should write it down." I ran to my makeshift office in the living room and began typing. About an hour past his bedtime, our son peeked out from his room. "Is it done?"

The entire story took less than an hour to write. To date, For the Love of Halloween is the only story that's come in a flash of inspiration.

The illustrations took years. But that's because fear kept getting in the way.

PM

P. Marin and her son in a photo booth years ago. That time he tried to scare her. Luckily, she didn't even scream or pee her pants.

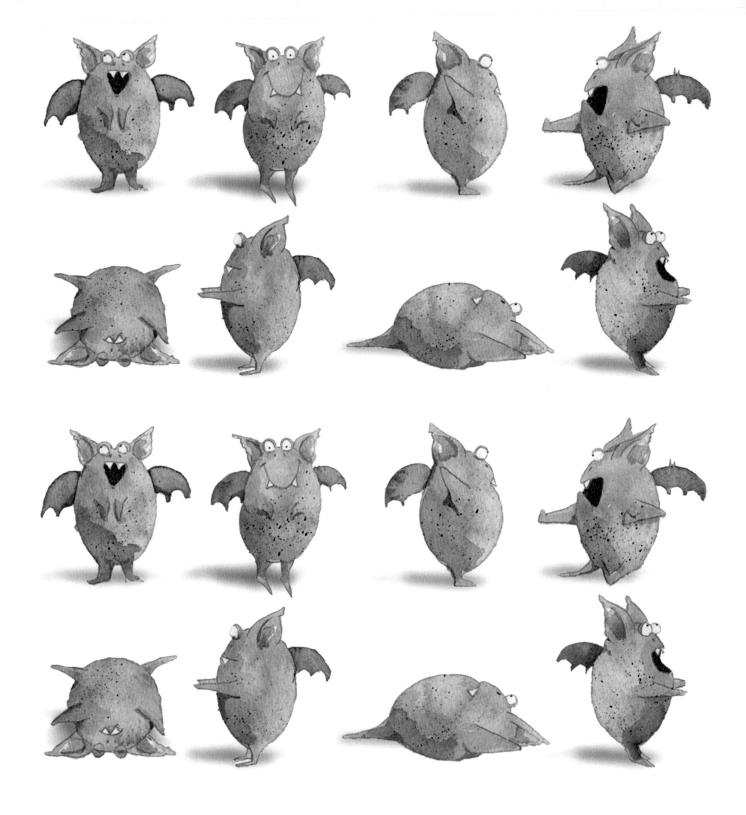

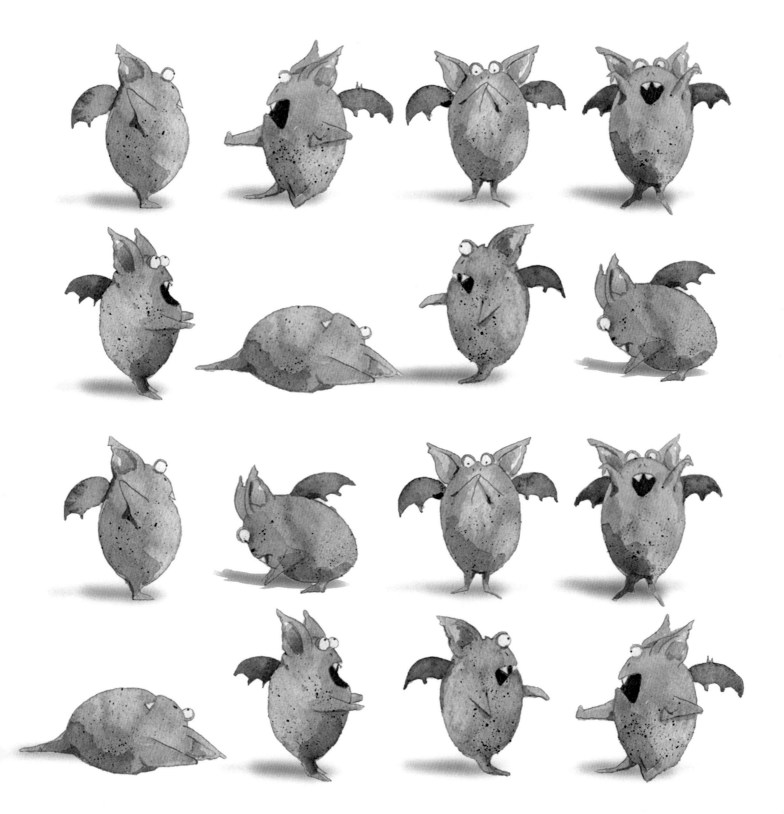

Made in United States
North Haven, CT
16 March 2023